For Sharmon, Nathene and Christine

PHILOMEL BOOKS
a division of Penguin Putnam Books for Young Readers,
345 Hudson Street, New York, NY 10014.
Philomel Books, Reg. U.S. Pat. & Tm. Off.
First published in 2001 by Hutchinson Children's Books Ltd., London.
Published simultaneously in Canada.
Printed in Singapore.   First American edition published 2001.
Text set in 20-point GUMDROPS-Old Style
Library of Congress Cataloging-in-Publication Data available upon request
L.C. Number 00-066590
ISBN 0-399-23709-7
1 3 5 7 9 10 8 6 4 2
First Impression

Old Bear's
Surprise
Painting

JANE HISSEY

Philomel Books New York

Old Bear had been busy all afternoon painting a picture.

"My painting of Little Bear will fit nicely in this tiny frame," he said.

"I want to
paint a picture
too," said Little Bear. "Are there any more frames?"
"There's a big one," said Old Bear. "Why don't you
and the others paint a picture together?"

"I want to do my *own* painting," said Little Bear, "all by myself."

"So do I," said Rabbit.

"And me," barked Ruff.

"Old Bear could choose one to go in the big frame,"
said Jolly Tall. "But what shall we paint?"

"I think I'll paint a ball," said Ruff, "or a spaceship or maybe a house . . ."

"Or just a pattern," suggested Little Bear.

"Why don't we *all* do patterns," said Rabbit. "I think I'll paint stripes."

He dipped two brushes into the paint and bounced along the paper, painting lines as he went.

"Oh dear!" he sighed when he reached the end. "My stripes are all wavy."

"That's because you bounce up and down when you run," laughed Bramwell Brown.

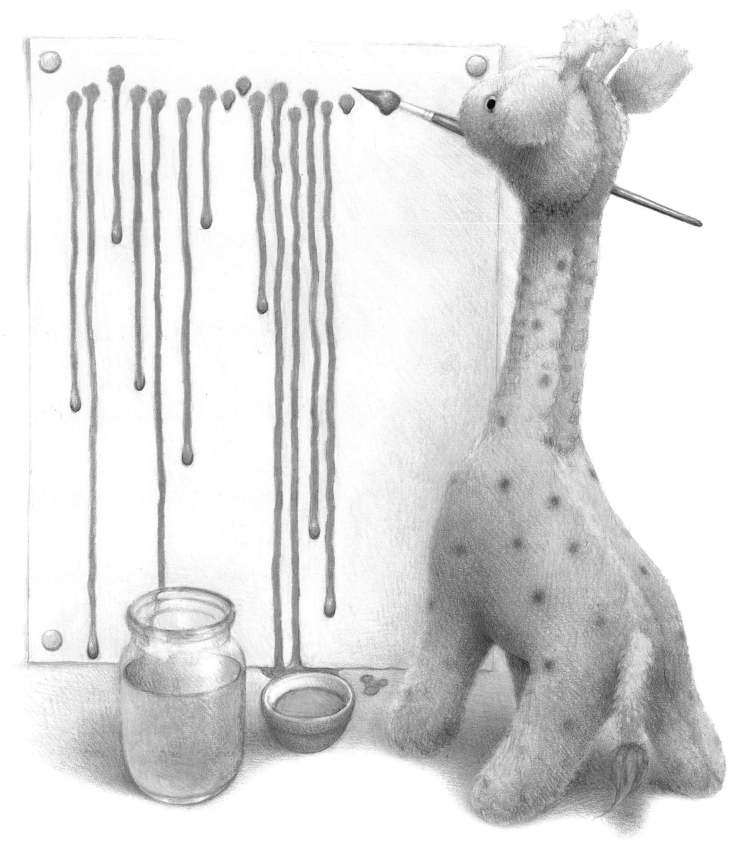

Meanwhile, Jolly had painted a row of orange dots.
"This is my spotty pattern," he said proudly.

But the paint was much too runny, and it dribbled all the way down the paper.

"Your spots have turned into stripes," said Rabbit. "And they're straighter stripes than mine."

Little Bear was waving his paintbrush above his head.
"Look," he cried, "I can make hundreds of spots.
My paper is covered in them."
"And so are you," laughed the other toys.

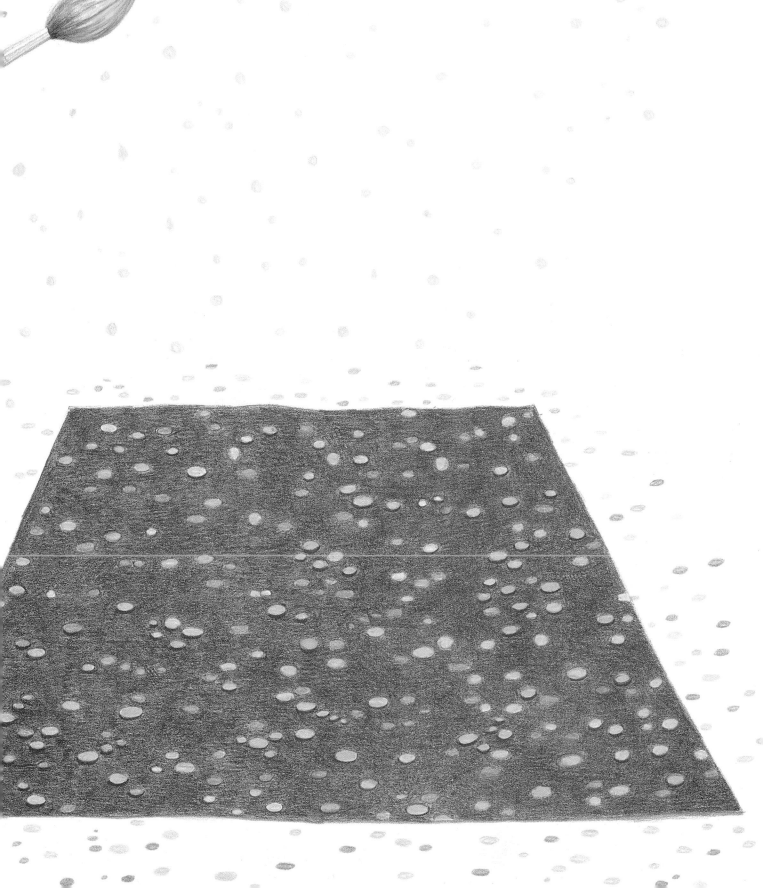

"I'm doing GIANT spots," barked Ruff.
He bounced his rubber ball into the paint
pot, then onto the paper.
SPLODGE.
It made a big splattered blob of yellow.

"That's fun," cried Little Bear. "Do it again."
But this time the ball missed the paper and landed
SPLASH in the water.

"Now there are puddles all over my painting," cried Duck.

"Sorry," said Ruff, dabbing the splashes with a cloth. "There, is that better?"

"It isn't quite the pattern I wanted," grumbled Duck.

"Well, I think all of the patterns are lovely," said Old Bear.

"I don't think they're so lovely," said Duck, staring at the dribbles and splodges and wiggly lines.

"Just wait and see," said Old Bear, hurrying away.

Soon Old Bear came back to collect the other toys.
"Cover your eyes and come with me. I have something
to show you," he said.

They arrived at a picture propped against the wall.

"Now you can look," said Old Bear.
"Oh, it's wonderful!" cried
Little Bear. "Who did it?"

"You all did," laughed Old Bear. "I just stuck your patterns together. Look, Jolly's orange stripes are the boat and Rabbit's wavy lines are the sea."

"Ruff's yellow splodge is the sun," said Duck, "and I must have painted the sky."

"I can see my spots," cried Little Bear, "on the sails of the boat." "That's right," said Old Bear, "and you all did the patterns on the fish."

"I see," said Little Bear. "So we did do an all-together painting after all. That was fun!"

"I said it would be," laughed Old Bear. "And now, let's have an all-together tea."

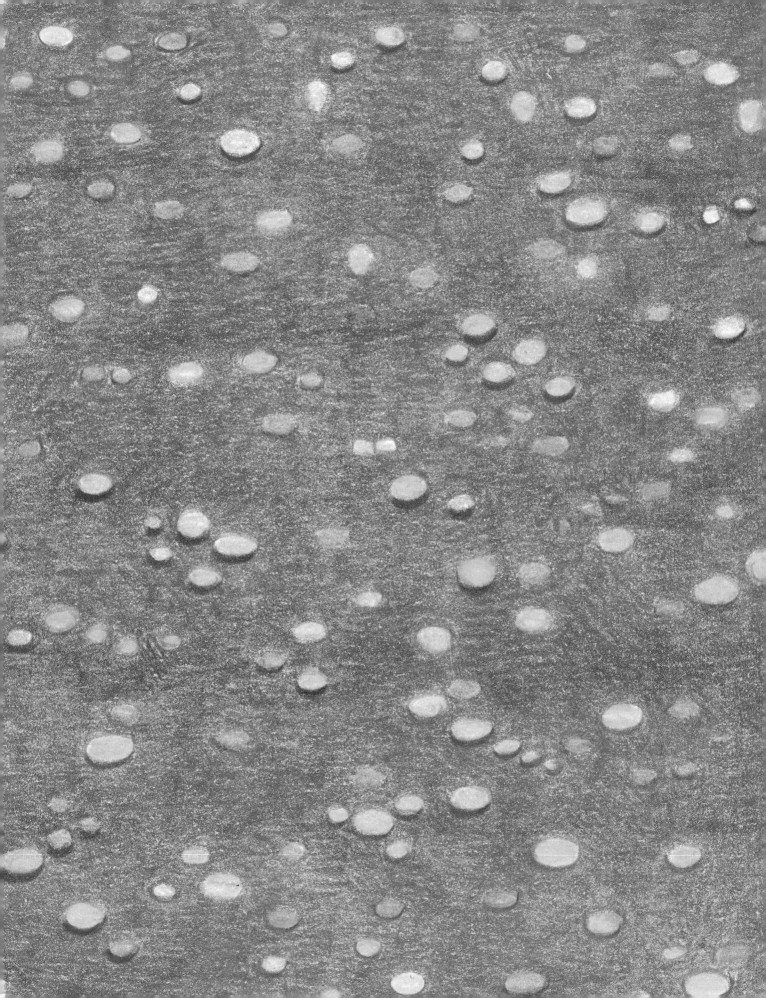